DIPLODOCUS

Titles in the Dinosaur Profiles series include:

DINOSAUR PROFILES

DIPLODOCUS

Text by Fabio Marco Dalla Vecchia
Illustrations by Leonello Calvetti and Luca Massini

BLACKBIRCH PRESS

An imprint of Thomson Gale, a part of The Thomson Corporation

THOMSON

GALE

Detroit • New York • San Francisco • New Haven, Conn. • Waterville, Maine • London

✦ *For more information, contact*
·The Gale Group, Inc.
27500 Drake Rd.
Farmington Hills, MI 48331-3535
Or you can visit our Internet site at http://www.gale.com

Computer illustrations 3D and 2D: Leonello Calvetti and Luca Massini

Photographs: pages 20-21 Louie Psihoyos/CORBIS; page 21 Hulton-Deutsch Collection/CORBIS

LIBRARY OF CONGRESS CATALOGING-IN-PUBLICATION DATA

Dalla Vecchia, Fabio Marco.
Diplodocus / text by Fabio Marco Dalla Vecchia ; illustrations by Leonello Calvetti and Luca Massini.
    p. cm.—(Dinosaur profiles)
Includes bibliographical references and index.
ISBN-13: 978-1-4103-0734-7 (hardcover)
ISBN-10: 1-4103-0734-4 (hardcover)
1. Diplodocus—Juvenile literature. 2. Dinosaurs—Evolution—Juvenile literature. I. Calvetti, Leonello, ill. II. Massini, Luca, ill. III. Title.

QE862.S3D394 2007
567.913--dc22
                                                          2006103260

CONTENTS

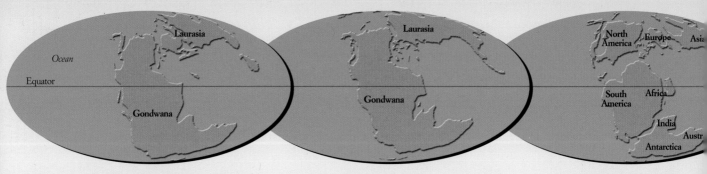

Late Triassic
228–206 million years ago

Early Jurassic
206–176 million years ago

Middle Jurassic
176–161 million years ago

A Changing World

Earth's long history began 4.6 billion years ago. Dinosaurs are some of the most fascinating animals from the planet's long past.

The word *dinosaur* comes from the word *dinosauria*. This word was invented by the English scientist Richard Owen in 1842. It comes from two Greek words, *deinos* and *sauros*. Together, these words mean "terrifying lizard."

The dinosaur era, also called the Mesozoic era, lasted from 228 million years ago to 65 million years ago. It is divided into three periods. The first, the Triassic period, lasted 42 million years. The second, the Jurassic period, lasted 61 million years. The third, the Cretaceous period, lasted 79 million years. Dinosaurs ruled the world for a huge time span of 160 million years.

Like dinosaurs, mammals appeared at the end of the Triassic period. During the time of dinosaurs, mammals were small animals the size of a mouse. Only after dinosaurs became extinct did mammals develop into the many forms that exist today. Humans never met Mesozoic dinosaurs. The dinosaurs were gone nearly 65 million years before humans appeared on Earth.

Late Jurassic
1–144 million years ago

Early Cretaceous
144–100 million years ago

Late Cretaceous
100–65 million years ago

Dinosaurs changed in time. Stegosaurus and
Brachiosaurus no longer existed when
Tyrannosaurus and Triceratops
appeared 75 million years
later.

The dinosaur world was
different from today's world.
The climate was warmer, with few extremes. The position of
the continents was different. Plants were constantly
changing, and grass did not even exist.

A Very Long Neck and Tail

Diplodocus is one of the few dinosaurs of which nearly complete skeletons have been found. Its closest relatives were Apatosaurus and the rare Barosaurus. All of these dinosaurs had very long necks. The neck of Diplodocus was around 27 feet (8m) long. Its tail was of even greater length—about 45 feet (14m). That is longer than a school bus!

The name *Diplodocus* comes from the Greek and means "double beam." This dinosaur was named for some unusual bones on the underside of its tail. These bones, called chevrons, were arranged in pairs. Each one looks a little like an upside-down letter T.

Diplodocus was one of the longest land animals that ever lived.

An adult could be as much as 90 feet (27m) long. It could weigh from 10 to 20 tons (9 to 18 metric tons). Besides its long neck and tail, it had four sturdy legs. The front legs were shorter than the back legs.

Diplodocus lived in the late Jurassic period between 155 and 148 million years ago. Remains of Diplodocus have been found in what are today New Mexico, Utah, Wyoming, and Montana.

This map shows what is today western North America in the late Jurassic period. The brown areas show mountains. The red dots show places where Diplodocus fossils have been discovered.

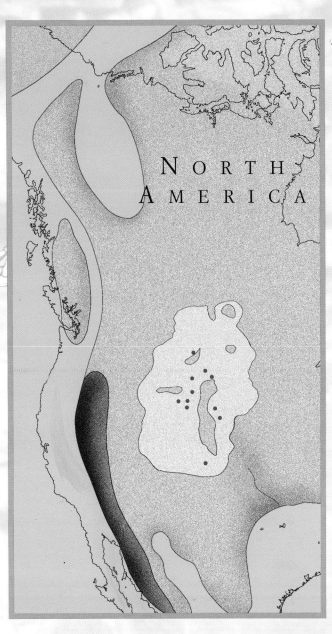

NORTH AMERICA

Diplodocus Babies

No Diplodocus nests, eggs, or young have ever been discovered. But paleontologists (scientists who study dinosaurs) have found many nests, eggs, and young of Apatosaurus, a close relative of Diplodocus. Diplodocus nests, eggs, and babies were likely similar to those of Apatosaurus.

The nests were probably covered with a mass of plant materials. As these plant materials broke down, they produced heat that kept the eggs warm until they hatched. A baby Diplodocus was about 3 feet (1m) long with a large head, a short snout, and enormous eyes. It grew rapidly at first and then more slowly throughout its life. It was nearly full-size by the time it was 7 to 10 years old.

FINDING FOOD

Diplodocus was a plant-eating dinosaur. During dry seasons when plant life became scarce, Diplodocus probably traveled to wetter areas where there was more food. These dinosaurs needed to eat huge amounts of food every day. When they ate up all the plants in one place, they had to move to another.

A Leafy Diet

Diplodocus had thin teeth shaped like pegs. It had only a few teeth, and they were in the front of the mouth. Scientists think this dinosaur used its teeth to strip leaves from branches. Diplodocus swallowed its food whole, without chewing. It may have swallowed stones that stayed in its stomach and helped grind its food.

TRAPPED

During dry seasons, lakes in the places where Diplodocus lived partly dried up. This created wide, muddy flats. A Diplodocus that made its way into one of these flats could get stuck in the mud. If it was unable to free itself, it starved to death. Predators who wanted to feed on trapped animals sometimes became trapped themselves.

In Wyoming, paleontologists discovered one of these mud flats that had turned to hard rock over millions of years. There, they found dozens of dinosaur skeletons, including Diplodocus, Camarasaurus, Apatosaurus, and Barosaurus.

THE DIPLODOCUS BODY

Diplodocus had a small, slender skull. Scientists have long believed that its nostrils were high up on its forehead, near the eyes. Today, though, some scientists think this idea is wrong. They think the nostrils were closer to the mouth. If they are right, the Diplodocus's head may have looked something like that of a horse.

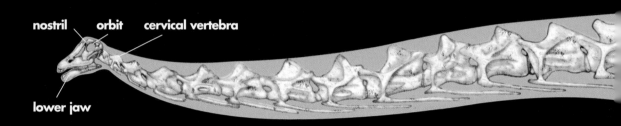

nostril   orbit   cervical vertebra

lower jaw

Diplodocus had thick legs like columns to support its huge body. The front feet had five toes like an elephant's. One of these toes had a large, pointed claw. The claw was probably used for defense. The back feet also had five toes, but they had two claws instead of one.

Besides being long, the Diplodocus's tail was slender. It could be swung like a whip and may even have made a sound like a whip cracking. The tail was probably used for defense or to attract a mate.

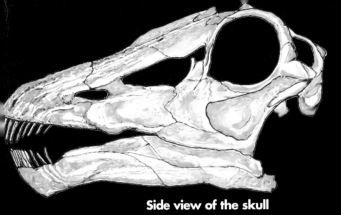

Side view of the skull

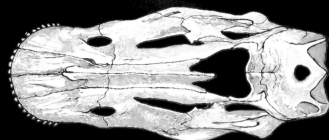

View of the skull from above

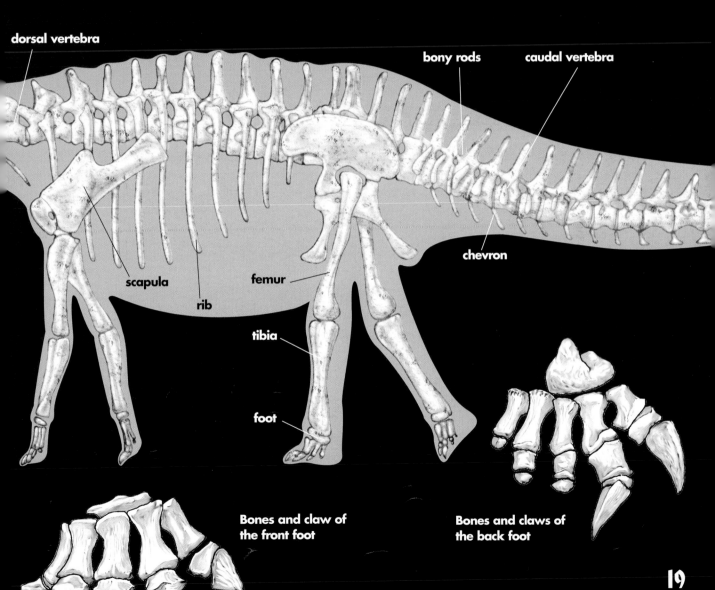

dorsal vertebra

bony rods

caudal vertebra

scapula

femur

rib

chevron

tibia

foot

Bones and claw of the front foot

Bones and claws of the back foot

19

Digging Up Diplodocus

The first few Diplodocus bones were found in 1877 near Cañon City, Colorado. In 1899, millionaire Andrew Carnegie decided he wanted a dinosaur to put in his museum in Pittsburgh, Pennsylvania. He hired people to search for dinosaurs in Wyoming. These workers found part of a Diplodocus skeleton later that year.

The next year, another part of a skeleton was found, along with some other bones. Scientists put the bones from both skeletons together to make one nearly complete skeleton. The finished skeleton was placed in the Carnegie Museum in Pittsburgh. It is still on display there today.

Plaster copies were made of the Diplodocus skeleton. This allowed models of the skeleton to be made and displayed in museums all over the world.

Another Diplodocus skeleton is displayed in the Denver Museum of Nature and Science. And Diplodocus bones, along with bones of many other dinosaurs, are preserved in a cliff face at Dinosaur National Monument in Colorado and Utah.

Above: **This display shows the si** of a human skeleton compared **t** that of a Diplodocus. It is in the Senckenberg Nature Museum in Frankfurt, Germany.

Right: Workers put together a model of a
Diplodocus at the Natural History Museum in
London.

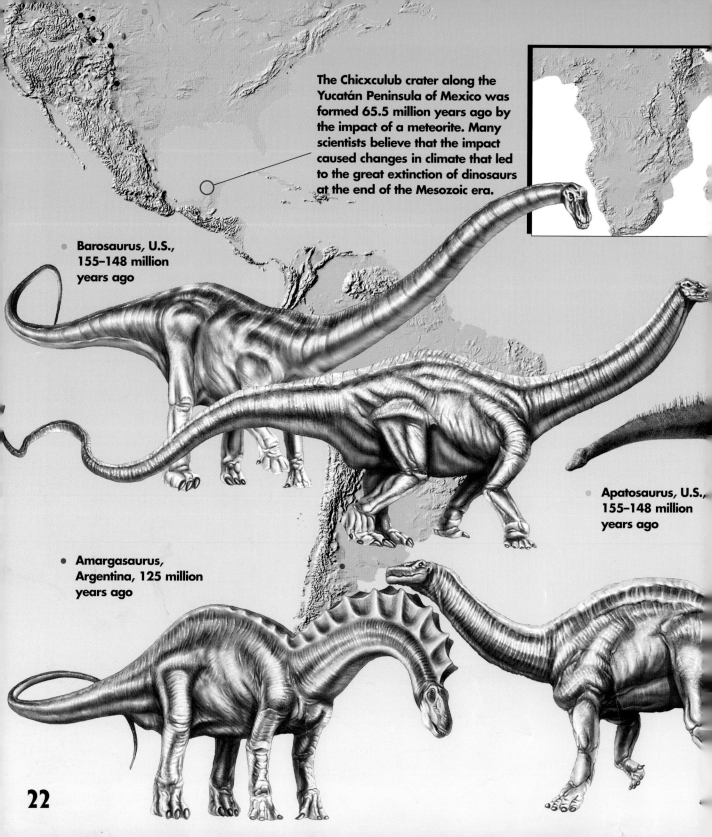

The Chicxculub crater along the Yucatán Peninsula of Mexico was formed 65.5 million years ago by the impact of a meteorite. Many scientists believe that the impact caused changes in climate that led to the great extinction of dinosaurs at the end of the Mesozoic era.

Barosaurus, U.S., 155–148 million years ago

Apatosaurus, U.S., 155–148 million years ago

Amargasaurus, Argentina, 125 million years ago

DIPLODOCOIDS

The diplodocoids were a kind of sauropod. They include Dicraeosaurus and Amargasaurus as well as Diplodocus, Apatosaurus, and Barosaurus.

Left: This map shows sites where the diplodocoids pictured below have been found.

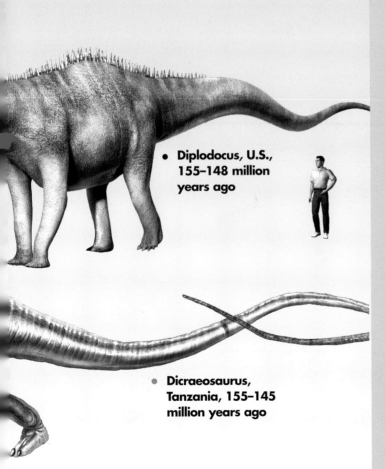

● Diplodocus, U.S., 155–148 million years ago

● Dicraeosaurus, Tanzania, 155–145 million years ago

THE GREAT EXTINCTION

Sixty-five million years ago, 80 million years after the time of Diplodocus, dinosaurs became extinct. This may have happened because a large meteorite struck Earth. A wide crater caused by a meteorite 65 million years ago has been located along the coast of the Yucatán Peninsula in Mexico. The impact of the meteorite would have produced an enormous amount of dust. This dust would have stayed suspended in the atmosphere and blocked sunlight for a long time. A lack of sunlight would have caused a drastic drop in Earth's temperature and killed plants. The plant-eating dinosaurs would have died, starved and frozen. As a result, meat-eating dinosaurs would have had no prey and would also have starved.

Some scientists believe dinosaurs did not die out completely. They think that birds were feathered dinosaurs that survived the great extinction. That would make the present-day chicken and all of its feathered relatives descendants of the large dinosaurs.

THE EVOLUTION OF DINOSAURS

The oldest dinosaur fossils are 220–225 million years old and have been found mainly in South America. They have also been found in Africa, India, and North America. Dinosaurs probably evolved from small and nimble bipedal reptiles like the Triassic Lagosuchus of Argentina. Dinosaurs were able to rule the world because their legs were held directly under the body, like those of modern mammals. This made them faster and less clumsy than other reptiles.

Since 1887, dinosaurs have been divided into two groups based on the structure of their hips. Saurischian dinosaurs had hips shaped like those of modern lizards. Ornithischian dinosaurs had hips shaped like those of modern birds.

Triceratops is one of the ornithischian dinosaurs, whose hip bones (inset) are shaped like those of modern birds.

24

Tyrannosaurus is in the saurischian group of dinosaurs, whose hip bones (inset) are shaped like those of modern lizards.

There are two main groups of saurischians. One group is sauropodomorphs. This group includes sauropods, such as Brachiosaurus. Sauropods ate plants and were quadrupedal, meaning they walked on four legs. The other group of saurischians, theropods, includes bipedal meat-eating predators. Some paleontologists believe birds are a branch of theropod dinosaurs.

Ornithischians are all plant eaters. They are divided into three groups. Thyreophorans include the quadrupedal stegosaurians, including Stegosaurus, and ankylosaurians, including Ankylosaurus. The other two groups are ornithopods, which includes Edmontosaurus and marginocephalians.

A Dinosaur's Family Tree

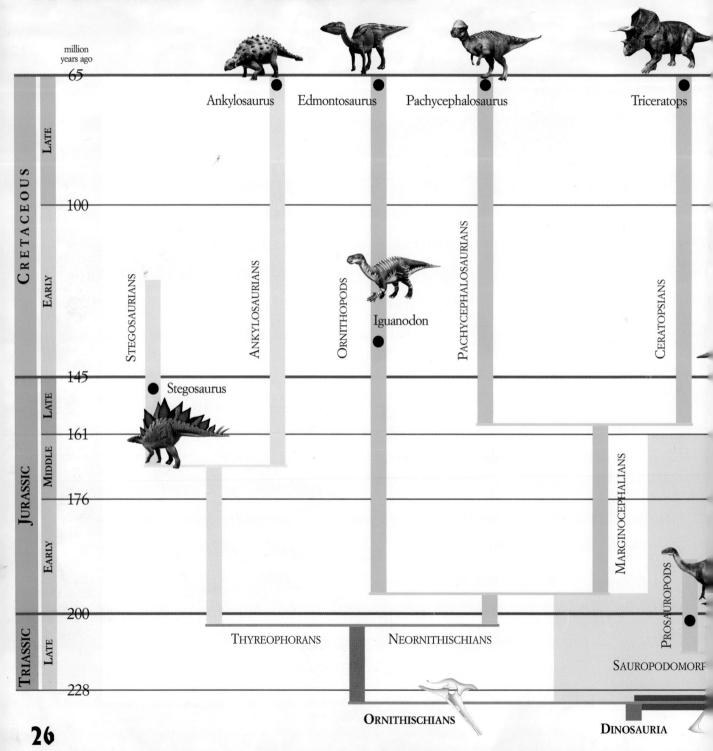

million years ago

CRETACEOUS

JURASSIC

TRIASSIC

LATE

EARLY

LATE

MIDDLE

EARLY

LATE

65

100

145

161

176

200

228

Ankylosaurus

Edmontosaurus

Pachycephalosaurus

Triceratops

STEGOSAURIANS

ANKYLOSAURIANS

ORNITHOPODS

Iguanodon

PACHYCEPHALOSAURIANS

CERATOPSIANS

Stegosaurus

MARGINOCEPHALIANS

PROSAUROPODS

THYREOPHORANS

NEORNITHISCHIANS

SAUROPODOMORF

ORNITHISCHIANS

DINOSAURIA

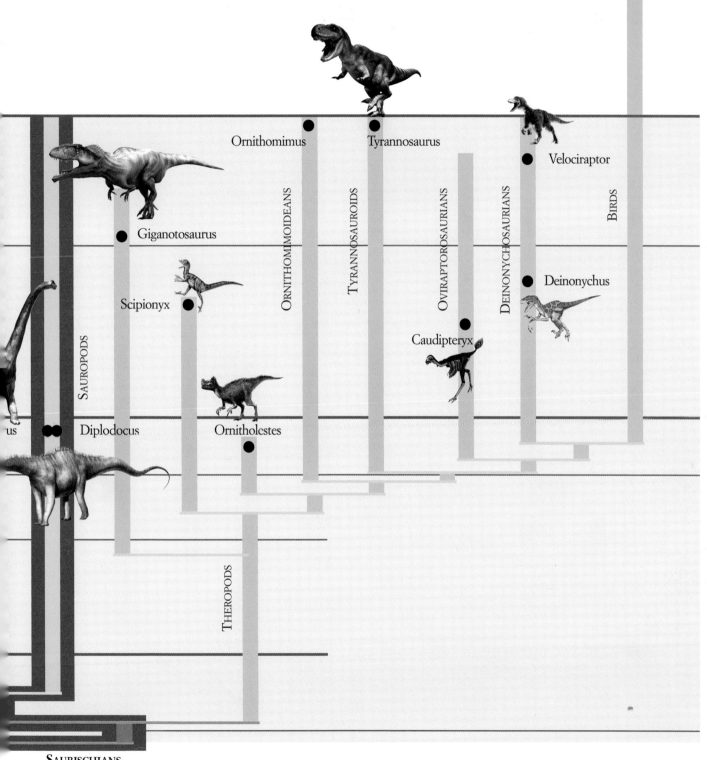

Tyrannosaurus

Ornithomimus

Velociraptor

Giganotosaurus

ORNITHOMIMOIDEANS

TYRANNOSAUROIDS

OVIRAPTOROSAURIANS

DEINONYCHOSAURIANS

BIRDS

Deinonychus

Scipionyx

SAUROPODS

Caudipteryx

us Diplodocus

Ornitholestes

THEROPODS

SAURISCHIANS

Glossary

Bipedal moving on two feet

Caudal related to the tail

Cervical related to the neck

Claws sharp, pointed nails on the fingers and toes of predators

Cretaceous period the period of geological time between 144 and 65 million years ago

Dorsal related to the back

Evolution changes in living things over time

Femur thigh bone

Fossil part of a living thing, such as a skeleton or leaf imprint, that has been preserved in Earth's crust from an earlier geological age

Jurassic period the period of geological time between 206 and 144 million years ago

Mesozoic era the period of geological time between 228 and 65 million years ago

Meteorite a piece of iron or rock that falls to Earth from space

Orbit the opening in the skull surrounding the eye

Paleontologist a scientist who studies prehistoric life

Predator an animal that hunts other animals for food

Prey an animal that is hunted by other animals for food

Quadrupedal moving on four feet

Skeleton the structure of an animal body, made up of bones

Skull the bones that form the head and face

Tibia shinbone

Triassic period the period of geological time between 248 and 206 million years ago

Vertebra a bone of the spine

FOR MORE INFORMATION

Books

Daniel Cohen, *Diplodocus.* Mankato, MN: Bridgestone, 2003.

Janet Riehecky, *Diplodocus.* Mankato, MN: Capstone, 2006.

Russell Roberts, *Where Did All the Dinosaurs Go?* Hockessin, DE: Mitchell Lane, 2005.

Web Sites

Dinosaur National Monument
http://www.nps.gov/dino/
This Web site maintained by the National Park Service features a virtual tour of a cliff face containing many dinosaur fossils.

Dinosaurs and Other Extinct Creatures
http://www.nhm.ac.uk/nature-online/life/dinosaurs-other-extinct-creatures/index.html
The Dino Directory section of this Web page created by London's Natural History Museum has information and many illustrations of Diplodocus.

The Smithsonian National Museum of Natural History
http://www.nmnh.si.edu/paleo/dino/
A virtual tour of the Smithsonian's National Museum of Natural History dinosaur exhibits, which include Diplodocus.

Walking with Dinosaurs
http://www.abc.net.au/dinosaurs/default.htm
The fact files section of this Web site contains information about many different dinosaurs, including Diplodocus.

ABOUT THE AUTHOR

Fabio Marco Dalla Vecchia is the curator of the Paleontological Museum of Monfalcone in Gorizia, Italy. He has participated in several paleontological field works in Italy and other countries and has directed paleontological excavations in Italy. He is the author of more than 50 scientific articles that have been published in national and international journals.

Index

Index